WARRIOR'S BREED

WARRIOR'S BREED

DEAN WILSON

J Merrill Publishing, Inc.
434 Hillpine Drive
Columbus, OH 43207
www.JMerrill.pub

Library of Congress Control Number: 2022922006
ISBN-13: 978-1-954414-66-2 (Paperback)
ISBN-13: 978-1-954414-65-5 (eBook)

Book Title: Warrior's Breed
Author: Dean Wilson

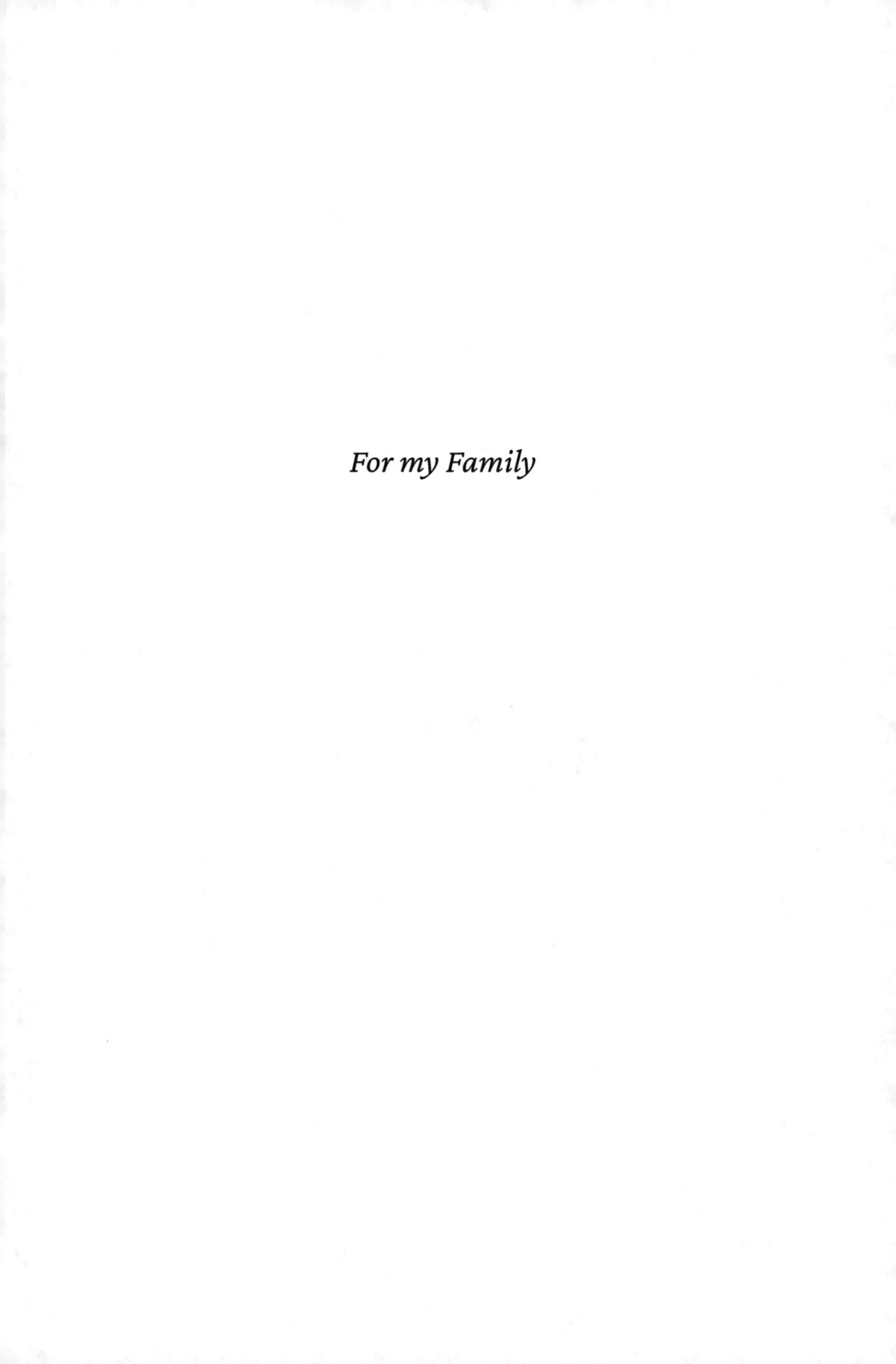

For my Family

CONTENTS

Safina's and Brahma   ix

1. The Love Birds   1
2. A Big Surprise   11
3. Back to Hell with a Mad, Angry Master   19
4. Half Hatched a Chicken Egg   27
5. Matchday and Escape Plan   39
6. The Sick Cock   47
7. In A Coma   53
8. A Meeting with the King   59
9. King of Prison   67
10. Human Injustice   79
11. Out of Coma   85
12. The Fight   89

About the Author   97

SAFINA'S AND BRAHMA

This book is a work of fiction about chickens who fight. No chickens were harmed in the making of this story. We love all types of animals. I have two dogs named Jack and Coby.

The story follows a simple and humble community of chickens, including fighting cocks and hens as their mates, whose homes were invaded and destroyed by humans. Many lost their lives, and many fighting cocks were captured in the struggle.

During the invasion, the main character, Toppa, was injured and lost his wife. She had recently given birth to a single egg, the largest the hens had ever seen. But she died protecting the egg with a broken wing and heart. As a result, Toppa became an evil and heartless cock, consumed by vengeance toward all humans. He was captured by a wealthy man who organizes illegal cockfighting events, where people paid top dollar to watch contestants from all over the world compete with their owners/trainers.

Toppa endured many wars, suffering, and physical and mental torture from his owner in his quest to become the best fighting cock in the world. His strength and desire for vengeance kept him going as he hoped to find his son, who may still be alive. Eventually, he decides to escape and make a run for his freedom.

Throughout the story, the birds question where the sense of justice is in a world where some animals are treated like kings and queens while others are treated as less than enslaved people. Birds were often kidnapped from their homes and used for sports or to make money for humans. Many were killed and eaten as if they were worthless. Despite dogs and cats being treated with respect, birds were often subjected to hardship and wickedness. Fed up with the excesses of humans, the birds no longer remained silent and chose to fight for their freedom.

CHAPTER 1
THE LOVE BIRDS

This story is about luck and second chances.

It was a rainy day, and although the old folks say rain is good luck, it didn't feel that way. We lived deep in the tropical forest, where the land was fertile and filled with beautiful trees that we slept in, with rivers nearby for drinking water. The leaves provided us a nest, and the ground and rotten trees gave us food we could easily scratch. It was the perfect home, and we all loved it.

Our ancestors, two cocks and two hens, discovered this place. Over the years, their numbers multiplied. We faced trouble from larger animals, but we were trained to escape by flying into trees and waiting for them to leave. We were very good at hiding. Rats were one of the predators we hated the most, especially regarding our young chickens and eggs. We also had to be wary of chicken hawks. When we heard a noise in the air, we took cover and hid until it passed. It was a hen's job to teach all her chickens about these dangers and how to hide or escape if they found themselves in such situations.

There once was a hen named Josette who had grown to maturity and was ready to choose a mate. When she was younger, she had always been interested in different things than the other chickens, and as a result, she had always been on the lookout for a suitable cock. Despite being approached by many suitors, she had always turned them down. However, one day, a stranger appeared - tall, well-built, and slightly different in color from the others. He was a handsome cock, and Josette was curious to meet him, as all the other cocks in the area looked alike.

As Josette tried to make her way toward him, two cocks rushed onto him and started to fight. But that was typical behavior for cocks. Every cock wanted to be the toughest and the leader. Everyone wanted to see what would happen, but Josette had a gut feeling that he was a warrior, and she was correct. He put those cocks down in seconds. He moved like the wind. That made her want him even more. She needed a strong cock to protect her, and all the other hens wanted him to.

To Josette's surprise, he looked at her, and their eyes met. He walked past all the other hens and approached her, saying hello. At that moment, Josette fell in love. He looked tired and dizzy, and then he fainted. Josette caught him before he hit the ground and hugged him tightly with her wings. He was so heavy that Josette struggled to bring him to her nest. She could tell by the look in his eyes that he was dehydrated, so she gave him plenty of water, bugs, and worms for protein. Then she told him, "Rest. We have a lot to talk about." He smiled and went to sleep.

Josette could hear a lot of chatter outside her nest, so she investigated. It was crowded with her hen friends who wanted to know everything about him and how they met. Josette shouted, "Calm down, ladies, calm down! I don't know him, but I always prayed to the gods that I would meet the right rooster of my dreams, and God just sent him to me. All of you stay away from him. He is mine, all mine. I've wanted little chicks so badly that I started to build my nest. But I couldn't do it without a rooster, and here he is now." She blushed and smiled with excitement. Everyone knew what she meant when she spoke.

As night fell, it was time for the chickens to roost. The cocks and hens flew up to their chosen tree to sleep, along with the hens carrying their eggs. The young chickens remained on the ground, nestled in their nests while their mothers kept them warm under their wings. Josette returned to her nest and cuddled up with her mate, feeling an amazing sensation she had never felt before. She wondered, "Is this what love feels like? I never want to let this go." Josette fantasized about everything she wanted to do and what she hoped her mate would do to her. She knew this was the start of a new life for her - a new experience filled with endless possibilities. Her thoughts exhausted her, and she quickly fell asleep.

Early the next morning, Josette heard the loudest crow in her life. Her eardrums almost exploded. No cock in the forest had ever crowed that loudly, and he kept going. "Are you feeling well, handsome?" asked Josette. "Yes", Toppa replied. "Thanks to you," he continued. "What's your name, beautiful, so I can properly thank you? By the way, I'm Toppa. My birth name is Toppabling. What's yours?"

"I'm Josette."

"Wow! Josette is a beautiful name for a beautiful hen," responded Toppa. "You're full of sweet talk," Josette replied. "Only love can get that out of me, princess," said Toppa. Josette was blushing and in the heat of this cock. She couldn't believe she found the perfect cock of her dreams. Josette's mind was thoroughly blown.

"So why are you speechless?" Toppa asked. "I'm sorry, I just needed a moment to take it all in," Josette replied. Toppa smiled and asked, "You love me? I feel the same. So, Josette, what will we do about it?" he asked. Josette was now playing hard to get, but in her mind, she knew if he held her, she would fall into his wings and give it all up with no questions asked.

"What brings you here?" asked Josette. Toppa replied, "Tragedy, my love. I escaped from some humans. They destroyed my hometown, captured two of us – my brother and I – put us in a vehicle, and took us away."

"What are humans?" asked Josette. "You don't know?" asked Toppa. "They are tall predators that love to eat chickens and look like monkeys without tails and hair. Some of them are as big as bears. They are the smartest creatures in the world, and they are cocky. Can you picture that?" Toppa asked Josette. "Yes, I can," replied Josette. "Well, they are the worst," said Toppa. "They have no good ones. They are all bad to me. They eat us and our eggs, and some of them take us to fight in games to make money. The one that captured us is a rich bastard. He has his arena and a place where they trained us to be the best fighters. In every fight, the loser dies. It's a fight to the death; that's how the matches are staged. I lost my brother in that same arena. These humans killed all my family. My brother was all I had left. I had many fights, but I won them all. I developed a fighting spirit that made me unstoppable. I worked twice as hard to be the best because I planned to escape to take vengeance on the humans. I was the best cock he had, and I made him millions of dollars. So, I know he will look for me. I battled cocks from all over and beat them all," said Toppa.

One day, some humans were taking cocks to a fight in a faraway town. Toppa watched as they locked the cages. On the way, Toppa managed to pull the lock on his own cage. He tried to free some of the others, but the humans caught him, so he had to escape. It took Toppa two days to find other chickens. He went through so much during that time, running nonstop, hiding, and fighting other animals. But Toppa's biggest battle was with a chicken hawk. The hawk came at Toppa quickly and tried to carry him away. Toppa had to grab the hawk and push his spur into its legs for it to let him go.

"I see your spurs are different," said Josette. "Yes, they're modified for battle," said Toppa. He continued, "They are my weapons. I was soaring until I reached a tree, then I hit the ground and started running." I heard him again; this hawk was not about to give up. Finally, I heard a voice say to stop, so I did. And when I turned around," Toppa paused. "What?" asked Josette.

"I was so tired and tired of running, so it was going to do or die. The chicken hawk was coming at me full-flight. I aimed and watched him carefully." As he caught up to me, I remembered my training. His feet stretched towards me, his claws open to grab me in a split second. I flapped my wings hard and launched my attack. I timed it perfectly, and with one clap of my spurs, I pierced his mouth with my spur. I saw blood splash on the ground from his mouth. He fell to the ground, and I went over to finish him. He started to beg for his life. I held back; I could not kill him. I told him never to trouble me again and that we could be friends." The hawk got up, "Thanks. I'm so embarrassed to be beaten by a chicken, but I owe you my life, he said."

Ok, are we cool?" replied Toppa.

"I asked the hawk if he knew where I could find chickens?" "Just over that hill," replied the hawk. "It's where we usually hunt, but those chickens are good at evading us." With great excitement, Toppa responded, "So there are more chickens here?" "Yes," Hawk replied. "But be careful because my boss is bigger and stronger," he continued. "Ok, thanks for the heads up," replied Toppa.

"That's how I ended up here, Josette," said Toppa. "Wow!" Josette replied in shock. Josette embraced Toppa. He could feel her love hardline, her heart pounding against him. Toppa was in the heat for her. Toppa started to sex her hard. Three rounds passionately, sweating, screaming, moaning, and groaning for hours. When they were finished, and Toppa gave Josette all his seeds, she held her belly and went to sleep smiling.

It was a month later, and Toppa had taught Josette how to read and write a scroll. He told her if anything should happen to him, give it to our firstborn son. Josette asked if Toppa could share the information and teach everyone in the forest. So, he did. Toppa taught them daily and even trained some of the cocks on how to defend themselves. But Toppa's most intense focus was on the scroll for his son.

The training exercises were going well, and when they heard a chicken hawk coming. They all started to run; even those Toppa had been preparing. Toppa stood there thinking he was about to face the same chicken hawk he had previously fought. But to his surprise, it was the 'big boss' he had heard about. The sun was so bright it blinded Toppa. Then the chicken hawk boss appeared before Toppa, blocking the sun.

Suddenly, Toppa heard Josette shouting, "Run, run!" But if Toppa turned, he would be dead. The chicken hawk boss was too close to him, and though Toppa was much smaller, he was ready for battle. When the chicken hawk boss reached for Toppa, he didn't expect what would happen next. Toppa quickly struck the chicken hawk boss in the face and caused him to bleed. The chicken hawk boss was furious. He turned around with rage, grabbed Toppa, and tossed him into a tree. Toppa's wing was broken. The chicken hawk boss approached Toppa and reached for Toppa's neck. Toppa used his left foot to hold him off and his right spur to pierce his head. The chicken hawk boss died on the spot.

Josette and the entire chicken kingdom watched in shock. Toppa was badly injured; he couldn't move. They all rushed to Toppa and celebrated him. Josette tried to pick Toppa up, but two other cocks told her no, they would help.

Toppa was in pain. The doctor applied some herbs on Toppa's wings; then the doctor tied them up for him. "I know this is a bad time, baby," said Josette, "but I'm about to lay my eggs." Josette could feel her eggs coming down. "So quick, baby?" replied Toppa.

Toppa was in pain but was also filled with excitement. The doctor told Josette he would watch over Toppa in his nest for the night while she went to her nest to lay her egg. "I fix up our hero," the doctor said. Toppa kissed Josette before two cocks took him to the doctor's nest. Though a celebration was going on in Toppa's name, he couldn't attend. The doctor's order was to rest and sleep.

CHAPTER 2

A BIG SURPRISE

Toppa woke up with a loud crow, which made him hurt. A hen told him that his girl Josette had laid a big egg. It was the biggest egg anyone had ever seen. The doctor and Toppa went to see Josette. The nest was crowded as everyone wanted to witness it. The doctor inspected the egg. Its color was different. Even the doctor was in awe. "This is the first time I have seen this," said the doctor. "Nevertheless, the egg was okay," he continued.

"Everything about you is different," the doctor said to Toppa. "You're a blessing in disguise." But just as everyone started to praise Toppa, hawk noises were heading toward them. Everyone was afraid and didn't know what to do. Toppa was injured, which scared them all even more.

"Hide, Toppa, hide!" said the doctor. "No, doc! Toppa replied in defiance. "They're here for revenge." The doctor headed into his nest to hide. Toppa didn't know what he would do, but he knew he needed to try, or all would be lost. Toppa stood there without fear and walked toward the body of the fallen chicken hawk. There were also two other hawks. To Toppa's surprise, one of them was the hawk called Billy, whom he had fought when he first came to the village. The other hawks asked, "Who did this?" Toppa replied, "I did!!!" "What? How can a chicken do this? No chicken has ever done this before," the hawks added. "I am from a warrior breed," said Toppa. "Now that the hawk king is dead, I am in charge," the newly minted hawk king said. "That was his wish, and now you all work for me. And now that I'm hawk king, I declare that no one will hunt here again, or they will die! Take the ex-king up and give him a proper burial," the new king said.

The new hawk king approached Toppa, "Now, I'm not only indebted to you for saving my life," said the hawk. "Because of you, I'm the one in charge. How can I repay you?" the hawk asked Toppa. "I want you to take care of my family. My wife Josette just laid an egg, and I know it's a son I will get. If anything should happen to me, it's your job to raise him. I will write a scroll to give to my son when he is born, so look out for it. I will get them now so you can meet them. "Anything for you," the new hawk king replied. Toppa called Josette and the doctor out of hiding. While waiting, Topped asked the hawk king how his beak was doing. "The wound needs to be cleaned," replied the hawk king. "Doctor, can you fix it?" said Toppa. Josette and the doctor emerged, and Toppa introduced them.

"Josette, this is the hawk I fought when I arrived here. He will ensure you guys are protected until my wings are healed." The hawk king once again promised Toppa that he would look out for his family as requested. The hawk king took a seat and the doctor so the doctor could fix him up. As Toppa watched the doc fix up the hawk king, Toppa realized he didn't know his name. "You never told me your name," said Toppa. "I'm Billy," the hawk king said. "Well, Billy, thank you!" Toppa said. "No, my friend, thank you," Billy replied.

The elder chicken of the forest soon summoned Toppa. They had a ceremony planned for Toppa. The elder honored Toppa, noting that Toppa was a legend and that many stories will be told of him for generations and generations to come. Toppa was humbled and grateful. After the ceremony and on his way back, Toppa answered questions from a group of chickens and cocks who questioned him training them. Toppa told them he could train as soon as he recovered.

It was two weeks later, and the chicken kingdom was doing well. There had been no troubles; everyone was doing their daily routines. Josette sat on her egg day and night, and her wing was healing superbly. The doctor monitored her daily. Billy the chicken hawk - Toppa's friend, would patrol. Everyone thought they were safe; however, destruction was ahead. Toppa took a walk deep into the forest to stretch his legs. He was accompanied by two friends, who kept a close watch over him. On these walks, Toppa would always give them exercises to build strength. Toppa taught them how to make dirtbags and use tree wisps to tie them to their feet to help build their stamina and give them strong wings.

Suddenly Toppa could hear chickens crying out for help. Though still in pain, Toppa took off as fast as he could. When he reached the chicken kingdom, humans were killing all the chickens. Then he saw the master, the one who had captured him. Toppa couldn't fly and knew he was the one they were searching for. "Because of me, everyone's lives are in danger," Toppa said to the two chickens accompanying him. "This is the moment I have been training you for. Muster up your courage, as your very existence depends on it!"

"One of you, come to my left and the other to my right. Hold me by my shoulders and fly stealthily toward that human up to his head," Toppa said. "Are you sure?" they asked with concern in their voice. "If I don't try, everyone will die for me, including Josette," Toppa answered. "Hurry, this is what I was training you for. Let's go!, shouted Toppa. They grabbed Toppa by his arms and flew as fast as they could, attacking from the back. As they reached the master's face, we attacked him from the back. When they got closer, Toppa's master heard the wings. But by the time he turned, it was too late. Toppa's spur connected him in his left eye, causing it to pop out. He was blinded in one eye. As the other chickens tried to escape, the master's men shot them all. Toppa's master grabbed him and put a gun to his head, then cocked the trigger.

One of his workers shouted, "No, boss! I know you are mad, but he can give us back the money to fix your eye and to make us millions. Don't forget the main purpose we are here. The master tossed Toppa to him and told him to lock Toppa up. Toppa glanced around for Josette and saw her on the ground, not moving. "Josette! Josette!" he shouted, but there was no reply. Toppa was furious and heartbroken, but he saw his son - the egg. Suddenly, Billy the Hawk showed up. He had seen what was happening from the air. Toppa shouted to Billy, "Remember your promise! There is my egg; raise him. The scroll is in the nest; teach him everything on it. Please, push him to the limit and train him hard to avenge me," Toppa continued. Billy replied, "I will!" Toppa was making a lot of noise, so the boss man knocked him out. The boss man and his people returned to the main roads where their vehicles were parked.

After the humans left the scene, the hawk returned to the nest, and all the surviving chickens ran away, leaving the bodies of the dead ones behind. Billy retrieved the egg and went to Josette's nest to get the scroll. While getting the scroll, he noticed Josette on the ground. Billy went to help, but she was still moving. "I'm dying," said Jossette in a faint voice. "Please help my Toppa and hatch my egg for me. And don't forget your promise; take care of our son." Josette took her last breath and then passed away.

"I will protect it with my life and teach him the scroll and how to fly," vowed Josette's lifeless body. "I will have my wife hatch the egg, and he will be the first chicken to fly fully," he continued. With the egg and the scroll, Billy set off. When Billy arrived home, he told his clan what had happened and all about Toppa and the egg. "With this scroll, I will teach Toppa's son well," he said. "If anyone even considers harming this egg, they will be executed. This egg will be our secret weapon. Who is with me?" asked Billy. "Hooray, hooray, hooray!" all the hawks shouted in agreement with their leader. "You have the hardest task," he said to his wife. "I already know what I must do," the Queen replied. "It will be my honor. Plus, this would be historic for all of us," she continued. "I love you, my queen," Billy said to her. "What would I do without you?" The queen smiled. As Billy walked off, he thought, "I just hope Toppa will escape again."

CHAPTER 3
BACK TO HELL WITH A MAD, ANGRY MASTER

When Toppa woke up, it was bright, but he could hardly see through all the bright lights. Toppa tried to move, but he was strapped down, and his bandaged wing felt numb. He saw shadows moving in the light. Then the light dimmed. Toppa heard them discussing his injuries and when he'd be back to normal. Everything was loud and clear, yet Toppa felt dazed. Then it dawned on Toppa, he was again stuck in the hell of the medical room. They pulled the straps and took Toppa to his cell, where he ate some grains and drank lots of fluids. He still felt weak and tired, so he went back to sleep. When Toppa woke up the next day, he took a deep breath. Training was in progress. There were many new cocks; some looked scared, some tired, and others resigned.

Pointing at Toppa, the trainer shouted, "That's the best cock here! " He is the world champion, and you all can be like him or better. While there is a new champion, Toppa has a heart. He never gives up. It will be an exciting showdown with these two," the trainer shared enthusiastically. The trainer woke up to Toppa's cage, "I can't wait for you to recover because only you can kill this cock." Toppa said nothing. The trainer continued, "He killed all his opponents, so you must learn new tricks. But first, you will need to heal." The trainer shared with Toppa that he knows he knows Toppa is angry, but he the trainer would look out for Toppa like he always did. "We both work for the boss, so I will do what I can for you," the trainer told Toppa. "I have all the other cock's fight videos for you to watch. I will get a TV so you can start watching." The new cock will be deadly, and the trainer wants Toppa to take this fight seriously. He also alerted Toppa that he overheard the boss saying he would kill Toppa if he didn't win. "They're betting everything on you, so it's all up to you," he told Toppa.

The trainer brought the TV and set up the DVD for Toppa. Toppa was able to see what he was up against. When they were finished, the other cocks went over to say hi to Toppa. "We've heard so much about you," one cock said. "We watched all your videos. You're the best," said another fighting cock. "Tell us how you do it. Because we can't prepare here properly. Whenever we have a cockfight, we lose two or three cocks. We will help you get well, and you teach us," said the cocks to Toppa.

"Deal," Toppa replied. "But when I am well, I want to escape this life. It's not for me. We all must fight our way out," Toppa shared. They all agreed. Toppa watched the new cock champion. He was from China, and he was good. He is light on his feet with taller legs than Toppa. Toppa would need to come up with some strategies to use against him. But first, Toppa's wings needed to heal.

Weeks passed, and Toppa was now healthy and fully recovered. Toppa was now trained at least three hours daily. When training was over, he would practice his new moves in private. Toppa wanted to have the best chance possible against this new champion cock. Toppa didn't need additional motivation, as his son and wife Josette were enough. Whenever he thought of them, he would train even harder. Toppa wanted to fly like his chicken hawk friend, so he tripled the weight on my wings and trimmed my body feathers.

The China cock was taller than Toppa, so he figured he would need to attack from above. So Toppa trained an additional five hours every day. After training, Toppa practiced flying like an eagle-like hawk for two weeks. It was difficult, but he mastered it. No chicken on earth could do what Toppa was doing. Toppa was proud of himself. Now, he could start practicing his airstrike moves. Toppa formulated the theory in my mind and then put it into action. It was all coming together perfectly. Toppa didn't share any of this with his trainer as he didn't want him to reveal what I had become.

It was one week to match day, and Toppa was ready. His trainer also thought he was ready and told the promoter he was pleased. "I better make back all the money I spent on surgery and the matches I lost because he was a no-show, and I had to go hunting for him," replied the promoter. "He better, or I will kill him," he added. "The China cock is good, but he will," Toppa's trainer responded. "He was now stronger than ever before and could fly like a bird," the trainer continued. Toppa laughed to myself. Toppa continued training but rested the last three days leading up to the big day. It was match day, and the fighting schedule was posted. There were ten cocks in the matches – the last cock standing would win. The area was jam-packed, with every seat sold out millions of dollars placed as bets, and all the top businessmen in the VIP section.

The ring announcer stepped up to the microphone and started to talk, introducing all the fighters by name. The crowd went wild. Everyone was placing more bets. The second fight was the China cock. The China cock wasted no time winning his match and quickly advanced. He steered in Toppa's direction, "You're next," he said after he killed the cock he was fighting.

Then the bell rang for Toppa's match. Toppa clapped his wings and knocked his opponent out of the ring. The crowd was shocked! With every win, Toppa and the China cock advanced one step closer to fighting each other. Finally, Toppa and the China cock were the last two standing. It was time for the matchup everyone had been waiting for. The crowd was silent.

Toppa was calm and composed. The China cock attacked first. His attack was strong and fast, and he was tall. Everyone cheered as he scratched Toppa's beak. Toppa thought of his son, which caused a rush of adrenaline to pulse. China cocked attacked, but Toppa quickly backflipped, hit him under his beak, and sent him staggering backward. Then Toppa took flight. The crowd was shocked. Toppa circled the China cock, preparing to give him the winning blow. Suddenly the China cock was lying on the ground out cold. Toppa was the champion again!

Toppa's trainer and promoter had smiled from ear to ear. In the heat of the moment, they gave Toppa a big hug. Toppa had just made them millions of dollars. "How did you learn to fly," the trainer asked Toppa. But Toppa evaded answering the question.

When the China cock recovered, Toppa went to him and asked if they could be friends. "T think we would make a great team," said Toppa to the China cock. "I could use your help. Can you meet me at the house so we can talk?" Toppa continued. "Sure," replied the China cock. "I was an asshole to you. I am sorry, and thanks for sparing my life." The China cock arrived at the house to meet with Toppa. "I am glad you could make it. I know, like me, you have a family. Don't you miss them?" asked Toppa.

"Yes'" Billy replied. "Every minute of the day," Billy added. Toppa told him about this plan to escape. "All these promoters do is use us to get rich; they don't care that we die. They killed my wife, and my son is out there somewhere. I must get back to him, and you have your family to return to, so let's do this together! I have a plan, but we will execute it in a month," Toppa told Billy. "But please stay alive, and don't let the trainer know," Toppa added. "Got it," Billy replied. The two shook hands, and he left.

CHAPTER 4
HALF HATCHED A CHICKEN EGG

The queen took the egg to her nest, where she had two more eggs. She treated Toppa's egg-like hers, overseeing it with love and tender care. Billy watched the queen - his wife, tirelessly sing and talk to the eggs daily.

There was a crack and another. The queen looked, and it was her two chicks slowly hatching. She called for Billy, her king. The news quickly spread throughout the Hawk kingdom. Soon the nest was full of people watching as the king's kids were hatched. The king was overwhelmed with joy!

Suddenly there was silence as the queen appeared in tears. The king held her. "He hasn't hatched yet," the queen said. "I did everything," she continued. But then everyone felt trembling. There was a whoosh, and Toppa's son burst out of his egg. The shell shattered like glass, with pieces of broken shell everywhere in the air. He was on the floor fighting and flailing like a free-style break-dancer. Everyone was amazed!

Tears of despair were now tears of joy. He was so feisty. The queen picked up Toppa's son and kissed him. "Welcome, my son," she said. She welcomed him to the family. "Your dad's name is Toppa, so we will name you Toppabling," the queen said. The crowd went wild.

Billy, the king, requested a banquet to be held right away. The king was happy eating, drinking, and speaking with his guards. The queen fed the kids many worms and grains before putting them to bed in their nest. Then she told her king she would be retiring for the night. "I'm tired, plus I have a lot to do with three kids, so I need to get my beauty sleep," the queen said. "I understand, my queen," the king replied. He hugged her, gave her the deepest kiss, and flew her to the nest. "Thank you, my queen," he told her. "You did well. However, our work has just started," Billy said to his queen. "But together, we can get through anything," she replied. The queen settled into their nest to sleep while Billy went to say good night to their kingdom. The queen cuddled up close to her babies, spreading her long, beautiful wings to cover them like a blanket as she fell asleep.

The king returned to the party. With gratitude, he thanked everyone for coming. The people cheered him. He quieted them a bit to finish speaking, "I need to take my rest, so enjoy the rest of the night, and please clean up after." Everyone cheered as the king flew away to his nest to join his queen.

As he flew towards his nest, he looked up to the stars and said, "Toppa, you're a dad; I'm a dad. I wish you were here to see our son's birth. I hope you're ok. Be strong, my friend, be strong." The king retired to his nest and cuddled beside his queen and chicks.

A month passed, and Toppabling was getting bigger and bigger. He was bigger than his brother and sister, but he also looked different. This bothered him. He often asked why he was so different. His brother and sister could also fly, and he couldn't, no matter how hard he tried. Toppabling grew more and more depressed and went to his mother crying. The queen his mom was cleaning the house when Toppabling burst in. "Mom, what's wrong with me?" Toppabling shouted through his tears. The queen stopped what she was doing and sat down. "We need to talk but let me get your dad first," she said.

The queen sent the guard to get the king. Within a minute, he was there. "Are you ok, my queen?" Billy the King asked. "I am, but your son is not. It's time for that talk," she replied."Oh, my son, you're almost fully grown now. I think you can handle what we are about to tell you; we just want you to remember how much we love you," Billy said. "What must you tell me, Mom and Dad?" asked Toppabling. "Calm down," the queen replied. They asked him to listen with an open mind. The king started, "My son, I am not your biological father, and neither is your mom. It all started when I met your father at the hunted ground. My son is a chicken that chicken hawks raise." The king told me Toppabling everything. As Toppabling listened, tears filled his eyes. "Son, your dad left me a scroll I will use to teach you. I have been digesting the contents within the scroll, I also promised to teach you how to fly. Use what we have told you to fuel your drive because it's up to you to rescue your dad. Plus, remember, we are here for you. Are you up for it?" Billy asked Toppabling.

Toppabling looked up at the king and queen (his mom and dad) with rage they had never seen before. He reminded them of when Billy and Toppa fought. Toppabling's response frightened the queen, and she started to cry. Toppabling didn't want to see her hurt, so he quickly calmed down. "Mom and Dad, thank you for everything and, most of all, for the truth. I knew something was wrong and was different, but now I know why," Toppabling said. "I need to meet my real dad. So, yes, I am ready for training. Plus, I so want to fly, " Toppabling said with excitement. The queen and king hugged him with much joy. "Let's go!" Billy shouted as he grabbed the scroll. "It's time to roll!"

The king kissed his wife, and he and Toppabling ran off to the teeing ground the king had prepared for this special day. A day he knew would come, and now it's here. He called a barber to groom Toppabling body hair. Toppabling got a very low cut, yet they didn't touch a feather on his wings. After grooming, the king had Toppabling lifting weights, doing pull-ups, and bench presses. The training was intense, but Toppabling used his grief to push on. He also learned to do in-flight one-on-one combat training with his dad. Toppabling's training was quite rigorous until he was able to master his flying skills. He had memorized and mastered everything within the scrolls. However, flying was still a challenge. So

Toppabling's dad added more weights to build upper body strength. Toppabling grew thick and big, and before finally developed the muscle strength to fly. His mom cried tears of joy. "I knew you could do it," she said. Toppabling's brother and sister congratulated him. "Now we can fly together. Let's race, they said with great excitement. "You're on," Toppabling replied before they flew off together.

They flew around the hawk kingdom and over the sea. Flying gave Toppabling so much freedom. He was loving his new skill. After returning home, they had a big dinner. Toppabling thanked his parents again for everything. But he knew he needed to find his biological dad. Though the queen knew this day would come, it saddened her. "You don't even know where to look," she told Toppabling. "While that is true, I've got to try," he responded. "I can't rest until he is safe, and those humans will pay for my mom's death," he continued.

"Calm down," son! "You can't think straight when you're angry. So you always want to have a clear head. Your father's secret to winning a battle is always to have a strategy. So, let's do this the right way, " the King told Toppabling.

"I have already sent troops to locate your dad

and will outline a plan as soon as we find him," Billy the King told Toppabling. "Ok, Dad, that's great news," he replied. "Thanks, I appreciate it," Toppabling continued. The king knew this day would come, so they prepared for it as best as possible. But they knew it would boil down to a plan and execution. Toppabling kept training while they tried to locate Toppa.

The king gave Toppabling a gift. Toppabling opened the box. It was a pair of golden spurs made in the king's workshop. He wanted Toppabling to be safe, and so he made him promise always to wear them. The spurs were made of twelve perfectly designed razor-sharp feathers. Toppabling installed six on each side and thought to himself how much of a killing machine they would make him. The new weapons were gold and shiny and would also blind his enemies. After admiring his new additions, Toppabling headed out to the training ground to test them out.

Back in hell, Toppa was still trying to devise an escape plan that would work. Not only were he and the Chinese cocks best friends, but they were also two the best in the world. A fight with them would cost millions of dollars. However, a fighter would still need to work their way up. But with no one ready to fight them, they had some time off and tied on their hands to plan their escape.

News spread across the world about Toppa and the Chinese cock. They made ads to scout new opponents who thought they could beat Toppa and his friend. If someone were able to, they would make a fortune. Included on the poster was the address of the arena. The king's general Damian and his scouts were traveling and stopped at house water when they saw the ads. Damian thought the cock looked like Toppabling and thought he must be his dad. The address was on the ad, so they thought it wouldn't hurt to check out the address, especially since it was not far from where they were. He and his men headed off to the arena.

Once they were there, they surveyed the area. They spotted a ground chicken who was responsible for cleaning the floors. They flew down and quietly grabbed him for interrogation. The chicken was scared. "Don't eat me," said the ground chicken. He continued, "If the master sees you, you're dead. They don't like your kind because you eat their investments.

Don't you know that he is here?"

Scope the area inside out. Do what you want with him, except," Damian told his men. "The master will hunt you and kill you for his prized chicken... his million-dollar money maker," said the grounds chicken. "You talk a lot," the hawks replied. "If you help us, we won't kill you," the hawks told the chicken. "You got a deal," the chicken replied. "We want you to tell Toppa his son is alive and well, and he will be coming to rescue him," the hawks told him. "It's impossible to rescue the chicken in this place," the ground chicken told them. "What do you suggest?" the hawks asked. "You will need to take out the guards and get the key from the master to open the cages," the ground chicken told them. "The only other person with keys is the trainer. But he doesn't act like a chicken. He acts more like a human," the chicken elaborated. "Thanks for the information; we got it from here," said the Hawks.

The hawks brought the ground chicken back to the arena to get their message to Toppa. But as they were about to drop him off, a guard spotted them and raised the alarm. The guards fired at them, hitting one of Damian's men - who later distracted them so Damian and the rest could escape. Damian's injured man, with his last strength, flew inside the arena to find Toppa. With his last breath, he managed to tell Toppa about his son. As he passed out, the guards _ with bullets. Toppa was enraged hearing about his son and seeing what the guards did. He vowed to make his escape in the next match because he knew if his son came to the arena, he would lose him.

Damian and the others flew as quickly as they could to tell everyone, especially the king and Toppabling, that they knew where they could find Toppa. It took them two days to return home and deliver the message to the king and queen. They were exhausted. Toppabling entered as the room news was delivered. "Son, we have good news!" the king said enthusiastically. "Your father is alive," the king said. "Yes, he lives," Damian seconded. "We found where he is and lost one of our men. The humans have the place heavily guarded," he continued.

Damian told them that if they attacked without a plan, they could lose lots of hawks. He told them about a map of the place and some insider details they managed to get from a chicken they interrogated. He also shared that he thought they had a better chance if they waited until match day... As the guards would be busy and the chickens out of their cages. It would also be crowded, limiting the guards' ability to fire upon them.

"How would we know which day is match day?" The king asked. "We could watch a thing called television," Damian said. "What's that?" the king asked. "While looking for Toppa, we stopped for water at a human's house and saw the television on," Damian replied. "The ads were saying they're paying millions to anyone that can produce a cock that can beat Toppa. The lady in the house called a man to come to watch the television quickly. That's how I got the information from television, said Damian. We camp out in their tree and watch the television until a match date is set", Damian added. The king thought it was a brilliant plan and commanded his army to start preparations. While they waited for a match day to be announced, they used the map to create a replica of the arena for training.

CHAPTER 5

MATCHDAY AND ESCAPE PLAN

A few weeks passed, and a Korean cock had started climbing the leader's chart. Finally, an opponent that seemed worthy enough to fight Toppa. The two bosses met to discuss the details of the fight and a date was set with five million dollars on the line.

One day while Damian was getting bored of waiting, there was a news alert on the television. Toppa was set to fight the Korean cock. After waiting there for weeks, Damian finally got the information they needed. Damian flew out of the tree as fast as the wind could carry him back to the Hawk Kingdom. "A fight date is set!" Damian shouted as he flew into the hawk kingdom.

Back at the arena, training was in full swing.

Toppa and the Chinese cock were even more motivated to work out. "Match day is the day," Toppa told his friend. "I have a good feeling about our escape and that I will see my son soon," said Toppa.

In the meantime, everyone talked about how much of a strong fighter the Korean cock was, as he had killed several opponents. Rumors had it that they were raising him on steroids and cocaine so he couldn't feel pain. The trainer got footage of him fighting, so Toppa could better prepare for the fight. Toppa wasn't concerned, but a successful escape would mean he couldn't get injured. So pay close attention. He realized the only way to beat him was in the air, and he had to finish him in one blow. After watching the footage, Toppa returned to his training to devise a counter-attack strategy. He named it Death.

While they waited for match day, Damian would keep tabs on the news about the fight. He occasionally perched in the tree to watch television and listened keenly to what others were saying in the streets. Everybody was talking about the fight between Toppa and the Korean cock. One day Damian overheard two people discussing the fight. When one of the cock said he heard Korean cock is very dangerous as he had torn other cocks he fought into pieces. The other cock agreed, and he heard the Korean cock was being fed steroids and cocaine. "No matter how much you hit him, it doesn't feel any pain," one of the cock said.

Damian became worried. He had heard about how some humans feed chickens a particular food that makes them grow faster and bigger. He also heard those birds became stupid and never thought of running away until facing their death. The fact that humans could feed a bird something that would make it grow bigger showed how potent their medicine could be. If the Korean cock was being fed something to make it stronger and wicked, they should be worried about Toppabling.

Damian flew back to meet the king. "We have some big issues to worry about," Damian told the king. From the looks on his face, the king could see that something had Damian worried. "What is it, Damian?" The king asked in concern. Toppabling had just returned from training and was heading into the house when he overheard Damian's conversation with the king. "I think Toppa is in big trouble," Damian said to the king. He may lose the fight even before we can rescue him,"' Damian said. The king looked somewhat confused. He couldn't understand why Damian was saying what he was saying. "I don't understand. Can you explain more?" The king asked Damian. "My king, I learned they feed the Korean cock steroids and cocaine. I learned he doesn't feel pain," Damian said as he looked at the king worriedly. Silence prevailed briefly as the king thought of what to say. Toppabling was also curious to hear what he was going to say. "Toppa is a fighter from a warrior breed, and I know he will prevail," the king said. "I have seen him fight. I have fought with him myself, and believe me, he is not a bird that could be easily beaten. But to be on the safe side, we will have to adjust our plans to be at the arena hours before the fight starts," the king told Damian.

After hearing the king's response to Damian Toppabling though a bit worried was satisfied. Though he was done training for the day, he returned to train some more. He had told himself that he needed to train harder to save his father. The Korean bird could be a problem, but if he could train harder, he could take it out should it try to kill his father in the fight. Toppabling was committed to learning some more dangerous moves. He also practiced breaking an iron net because the fight would happen inside an iron cage. From what Toppaling had heard about his father, together, there was no obstacle they could not overcome.

"What were you discussing with Damian?" the queen asked the king. She had been so busy that she didn't have time to listen to the full conversation. "Damian told me that the Korean cock that Toppa would be fighting was being fed steroids and cocaine. This makes him more tolerant of pain and also makes him brutal. It is said that he has killed other cocks with ease," the king told the queen. A worried look came over the queen's face. "I am really worried about Toppa. He has been captive for a long time and has yet to meet his son," she said. "I just don't want anything to go wrong," she added. "Nothing will go wrong, my queen," said Billy the King. "I've already instructed everyone going on the rescue mission that on fight day, we will be leaving here as early as possible. We will get to the venue before anyone to watch the fight and ensure that if Toppabling is at risk, we will be there to assist," the King said. "That's a good plan, but it will still put some of us at risk," the queen complained. She couldn't help but feel that this time Toppa's life might be at risk and was worried if the fight was the right time for them to carry out the rescue. "Life is all about risk, my dear. But we must save Toppabling, no matter the cost," the King said. "Remember how he spared my life? I owe him my life, plus he is the reason I'm king," the king added.

Hours passed, and the king was looking for Toppabling. He would usually be home by a certain time, but he was not. The king became worried. "Where is your brother, Toppa?" the king asked his son. "He is still training," the king's son responded. "He was here about an hour ago but left again. I think he heard some of your conversations with Damian," the son told his dad. "I believe he's getting more training because he knows what lies ahead," the queen explained. "There is a limit to how much one would train. Too much of anything can be bad. He could break his wing or one of his legs, and if that happens, he may not even be able to join us in the fight," the king complained. The king then left the house searching for Toppabling and found his training. "It is alright, my son.

"Don't overdo it, or you will get injured," the king told Toppabling. "I just want to be stronger and better," said Toppabling. "I understand, but you still need to rest. You are overdoing it, putting you in harm's way," the king told Toppabling. "Saving your father is a priority, but you must get some rest. You are already stronger than I imagined you could be," the king continued. "I am just worried about what the Korean cock might do to him," Toppabling complained as he frowned. The king got closer to Toppabling, and in a comforting voice, he patted him on the shoulder, saying, "Your father is the best when it comes to a fight. You don't need to worry about that." Hearing this comforted Toppabling's mind, and together they headed home.

CHAPTER 6
THE SICK COCK

It's just two days before the match between Toppa and the Korean cock. Everyone was anxiously waiting for Damian to return the next day to give them a final briefing on how things were going. He had been returning to where he was watching the TV to keep up with the latest news on the fight.

The king and queen were eating lunch when they saw Damian flying towards them. They were surprised because he was a day early. This made them anxious. "My king, an issue has arisen," Damian said as he landed before the king and the queen. There was an inquisitive look on the king and queen's faces. "What is wrong, Damian?" The king asked immediately. "The Korean cock was rushed to the hospital. According to the news, the Korean cock and Toppa's match had been postponed until further notice," Damian disclosed. The king and the queen looked at each other in disbelief. They gazed at each other and then back to Damian. "Why was he taken to the hospital?" the king asked. "I don't know the details. He was rushed to the veterinarian after he collapsed during training," Damian said. "This is a setback for our rescue plan," the queen said.

"According to what they said on the TV, another date will be set," Damian replied. However, it will depend on how long it takes for the Korean cock to recover," Damian explained. "You must go back, Damian," the queen exclaimed. "You must watch the TV and listen to the streets. I need to know what's wrong with the Korean cock, and I also need to know the new date for the fight," instructed the king. "Go now!" He commanded Damian. "My king, I am hungry. Can I eat something before I go?" Damian complained. The king gave him a staring look. "It's alright, my king," the queen interrupted. "Damian, you can join us in eating, but you will have to return immediately after," she told Damian. With a look of excitement on his face, Damian joined them.

Later they found out what happened to the

Korean cock. Rumors had it that the Korean cock's master had an issue with the worker who was feeding him. The master had fired the worker a few days before and employed another worker to take care of the needs of the Korean cock. The new worker was responsible for cleaning the place the Korean cock was staying, feeding it, and giving it water to drink. If there was a need to give some drugs to the Korean cock, this new worker was also responsible. The Korean cock was also forced to sleep by noon. The Korean cock didn't like this at all, but its master had insisted that it must sleep at noon. According to the veterinarian professional, this would help them become stronger and bigger. These were the same veterinarians that provided the cocaine and steroids the master fed the Korean cock.

It was only a few days before match day, and the new worker was instructed to add cocaine and steroids to the breakfast of the Korean cock. Usually, they would add specific dosages of cocaine and steroids to the Korean cock's breakfast and dinner but not its lunch allowing it to sleep well without being much under the influence of drugs. However, the master had neglected to tell the new worker who was about to serve his prized cock for the first time.

The new servant prepped breakfast for the Korean cock, and added three spoonfuls each of cocaine and steroids instead of one spoonful each of cocaine and steroids. He then took the food to the Korean cock, who ate everything immediately because it was already starving because the worker did not bring the food as early as the old servant used to. Immediately after breakfast, the cocaine and steroids started reacting aggressively in the body of the Korean cock. Its head started spinning, causing it to stumble as it walked. With every stumble, he would hit its head on the edge of the cage. This severely injured the Korean cock was severely injured which started to bleed. He also injured one of its eyes, and some of its organs started malfunctioning. The cock was suffering from the effects of an overdose. It was having trouble breathing and soon after collapsed.

When the master of the Korean cock returned, he checked in on the Korean cock. As the master walked towards the cage where this Korean cock was kept, he saw it lying on the floor. At first, he thought it was sleeping, but then he realized it was not noon. Plus, the cock didn't like sleeping, so part of the worker's responsibility was to watch it while it slept for at least an hour. As the master got closer to the cage, he could see something was wrong. He rushed to open the cage and tried waking the cock, but it was not responsive with a weak pulse. The master was confused about what to do.

The match between the Korean cock and Toppa was just a few days away, and the Korean cock's health was in question. Typically, when a fighter in a pending bet match dies, there is always a fifty percent cut on the bet money placed by the master of the dead fighter. The remaining fifty percent is shared between the organizers and the opponent. However, an exception is made if the fighter is sick. The competition would be postponed until the fighter fully recovers. While the master of the Korean cock was still trying to compose himself, he realized the Korean cock now had no pulse. He was worried about how much money he would lose should anything happen to the Korean cock. He started performing CPR on the cock and did so for three minutes before the cock started breathing. He quickly carried the cock to his car and rushed to his veterinarian. The Korean cock was admitted, and the doctors ran a few tests. The doctors told the master that the cock was suffering from the effects of an overdose. It would have died of heart failure if not for the CPR which its master had performed on it.

CHAPTER 7
IN A COMA

Everyone was disappointed that the fight was postponed. Even the owners of the house where Damian watched TV were also disappointed. While everyone shared their disappointment, no one discussed why it was postponed. Damian was frustrated; he knew that the queen and the king were waiting for him to return with feedback as he had always done. Not even the news disclosed what happened to the Korean cock. The news also said the Korean cock was in a coma. Damian didn't know what it meant for someone to be in a coma. If he were home, he would be able to check a dictionary.

One afternoon, Damian was hiding at the top of the tree where he had been staying when he heard two kids discussing the match on their way home from school. He was baffled at their knowledge. "The Korean cock was taken to the hospital for treatment and has been in a coma since," kid number one said. Hearing this made Damian even more interested. Maybe this was his chance to get the information that he wanted. "What do you mean by being in a coma?" the second kid asked. "Being in a coma is when one is in a state of unconsciousness. They are alive but without being aware of their surroundings. They just lie there in a deep sleep," Kid Number One responded. "You know everything," Kid Number told Kid Number One as he smiled happily. "That's because my dad is a doctor, and he tells me a lot about what happens at his hospital," kid number one replied. The two kids continued with their discussion as they walked towards their destination. Damian was relieved to know what it meant to be in a coma finally.

Damian had a thought. Since humans were surely more intelligent and had technology at their disposal...What if some of the chicken hawks that died in their territory were not really dead? What if they were actually in a coma and they buried their comrades alive? Humans have larger and more organized brains. They have cars that take them from place to place and airplanes that help them to fly high in the sky. There was a time when Damian tried to go faster than an airplane, but he couldn't keep up or go as high. Humans even have TVs and electricity to power them. Humans were superior in so many ways.

One of the things Damian enjoyed a lot about human territories was the variety of foods they had to eat. Not to mention, they were also far more tastier than they had in their territory. Damian would look forward to whenever humans dropped crumbs of food. If they did, he would ensure it was safe then jump down as fast as he could to eat whatever they had dropped on the ground. Chicken hawks preferred to hunt cocks and hens, especially the little ones. Because they were easier to carry, and they were too weak to fight them off. There were times Damian and some of his friends used to go out to hunt on cocks and hens. Their meat was the sweetest thing they had ever eaten. Since Billy took over as the new king, they had been warned against attacking cocks and hens. This was challenging, but they obeyed, settling for lizards. The meat from the lizard didn't taste as sweet as that of the cock and hen, but they had no other option but to obey their king. Other hawks from other territories were still hunting cocks and hens, but they were loyal to their king. This is what separated them from other clans in all the Hawks.

Something else was bothering Damian. He still didn't know why the Korean cock was in a coma. He had never heard about a bird going into a coma. Sometimes birds in their territory died or were sick, and the king would ask the doctors to determine the cause. The doctors always had something to tell. Damian knew something caused the Korean cock to be in a coma. He wasn't sure how to get that information but promised himself he wouldn't return to give its king any briefings until he found out why the Korean cock went into a coma. Another two weeks had passed, and Damian remained around for two weeks and still didn't have the information he needed. The TV people didn't know what caused it. He listened to the conversations of those passing by, but no one around seemed to be discussing it. Damian knew the king and the queen would have had concerns, and it would be a matter of time before they would send someone to get updates.

Damian sat for a while, thinking of what to do and where to get the information needed. The only place that came to mind was to poke around where the Korean cock lived and trained – where it all happened. This would be risky. Damian thought back to how Kyle was killed when they went to survey the place where Toppa was caged. Going to where this Korean cock used to be kept would mean putting itself at risk, but Damian didn't see any other options. It was evening when he arrived, and some workers were still around. Damian quietly landed on a tree close to where some workers sat to rest and have conversations. Damian hoped he would learn something from their discussions. But he heard nothing.

The following day, two workers had come to sit at this spot. They seemed to be speaking in a low tone as if they were discussing something they didn't want anyone to hear. Damian noticed they had no weapons, so he felt safe to fly down and get closer to them. Damian got closer so he could eavesdrop on the conversation. He heard one of the workers telling the other the Koreans cock's new servant had been fired because the worker fed him the wrong dosage of drugs and caused the coma. Damian had finally gotten the information he needed. It was time to go home and brief the king about what happened. As Damian flew home, he saw pieces of food particles on the ground that humans had dropped. It was tempting to stop, but he remained focused because the king was waiting. Plus, too many people were around.

CHAPTER 8
A MEETING WITH THE KING

"We need to check on Damian; he has been away too long," the queen complained. "Maybe the humans caught him," Toppabling said. "No, Damian is very smart; I don't think they have discovered that he has been spying on them." the king said. "Humans hate spies and will go to any length to eliminate a spy," the queen said. "I have been training tirelessly and can't wait for when I can finally rescue my father," Toppabling said. "You will soon, but we have to wait to hear from Damian," the king said. "Mother might be right about something happening to Damian," Toppabling shouted. "They could have set a new date, and we wouldn't know because something could have happened to Damian," Toppabling continued. Toppaling was concerned that he would miss the opportunity to save his father. "I don't think so. My instincts tell me that Damian is..." While the king was still talking, one of his servants ran into the house, "Damian is approaching," the servant blurted out. Everyone was happy to hear this. Now they could get briefings on what was happening on the human territory, and they would know how to proceed with rescuing Toppa.

Damian exhaustingly walked into the room and approached the king. "Please sit. You look tired," the king said to him. Damian didn't hesitate. He took a few minutes to catch his breath while everyone waited anxiously to hear what news he had brought them. "A new date has not yet been set as the Korean cock is still at the vet," Damian disclosed. Everyone was disappointed. They couldn't understand what kind of sickness would cause a cock to be hospitalized for two weeks. They believed that birds are one of the organisms that recover quickly from whatever ailment would attack them.

"Are you sure this Korean cock is not dead?" the queen asked. She didn't see the possibility of a cock spending over two weeks in the hospital and wasn't the only one feeling this way. "No, he is not dead. They said he is in a coma," Damian shared. Damian could see from the expression on everyone's faces they were confused. After all, he was previously confused as to what the term meant. "Please explain what you mean by the cock being in a coma?" the king demanded. "According to what I learned in human territory, being in a coma means being in deep sleep as if one was dead, even though one is not," Damian explained. "One wouldn't be aware of what is happening around them or be able to open their eyes. According to what I have heard, some people sleep that way for nearly a year," Damian added. The queen, the king, and Toppabling were all in shock. "How is that possible?" Toppabling asked. "I was surprised too when I heard about it. Humans do not cease to surprise us with their intelligence," Damian said. "This is unbelievable," the king replied. "Yes, my king, but it is real," said Damian, who told them why he decided to stay longer to get the details.

The king and queen thought this was something their own doctors and scientists should start researching. "What if we had buried colleagues who weren't dead?" Damian asked. "This is so insane," the queen said in a concerned tone. "What did they say was the cause of the Korean cock being in a coma?" the king asked as he fixed his gaze on Damian. "That's why it took me so long to return," replied Damian. "I was trying to find the cause because I knew my king would want answers. Damian continued to explain that no one had answers, and if they did not, they weren't saying anything. He shared the lengths he went through to discover what had happened. "I decided to go where it all happened," Damian explained.

The king and the queen were shocked. "You mean you took the risk of going there alone?" the king exclaimed. "Yes, my king, I had no choice," Damian responded. "That's a very reckless thing to do. The last time you did something like that, we lost a loyal comrade," the queen complained. "At least I wasn't caught, and I was able to get the information I wanted," Damian quickly responded. A brief silence prevailed briefly before the king, and the queen replied, "You're right, Damian! Though they thought he was reckless, they were also pleased with Damian's efforts. "So, what did you find out?" King Billy asked. "The Korean cock overdosed on steroids and cocaine," Damian disclosed. "So, how did it happen?" The king asked. It seems that it was a mistake on the part of a new worker," Damian elaborated. "Overdose is always a bad thing. Even the drugs doctors give us here, if you overdose, they could kill you," the queen said. "Cocaine is a human drug. I don't understand why they were feeding it to this Korean cock," the king complained. "No wonder the cock acted like a mad cock. Tearing its victims apart. It was under the influence of steroids and cocaine," Damian added.

"Now we have a problem! We don't know when the next date is going to be. They may end up canceling altogether," Toppabling complained. "No one even knows if the Korean cock will come out of his coma," Toppabling mumbled. According to what Damian heard from the humans, not everyone survives a coma. Some die while in a coma Damian. "So now we have to wait and see if the match will be back on," the queen said. "I guess that means I'll need to return to continue eavesdropping on the humans," said Damian. "Last time you stayed so long, you worried us," the queen complained. "However, I don't think that should be an issue now because you must return only when you get information on the next fighting date. Once the fight is back on and a date and time are announced, you return immediately, so we can start preparing. If the fight is completely canceled, you let us know so we can come up with another plan to save Toppa.

After their conversation, the king asked Damian to spend time with his family before returning to the human territory. Damian complied. He had missed his family a lot. After Damian left the king's house, the king called for an emergency meeting with the head doctors and scientists. He gave them the details of Damian's discovery about a bird slipping into a coma. While they knew what come, they had never heard of or seen a situation where a bird slipped into one. They inquired about the cause, and the king explained that it was an overdose. Due to the cause, the doctor told the king it would indeed be possible that a cock could go into a coma caused by an overdose. The king demanded they do more research about it because it would be beneficial in strengthening their medical delivery. So they did as instructed.

Billy, the king, had a strong vision of building his territory to have health delivery. He believed that if they could improve their health delivery, they would attract birds from other territories. The health sector wasn't the only thing the king wanted to improve. He also wanted to improve the standard of living of his citizens. The king had made education compulsory for every child living in the territories. Parents who refused to send their children to school would be fined a percentage of their food. No bird wanted to be fined. They ate a lot and didn't have enough to keep their stomachs full. Giving away some of their food was something they wouldn't want to do, so they did their best to avoid being fined. They made sure they sent their kids to school. The king always preferred to find his subjects ' food materials and didn't want to have to find anyone. But, this was the easiest way to get everyone to comply easily with the territory's laws. The food fine was adopted as the offense for most wrongdoings committed. However, this was only for lesser offenses.

The following day, Damian bid farewell to his family. He then visited the king before leaving for his assignment.

CHAPTER 9
KING OF PRISON

One thing about success is that everyone wants it or at least wants to identify with one who is. This was what Toppa was experiencing. The Chinese cock was like his closest friend in the habitat. The other cocks and hens wanted to be associated with Toppa because of his success. He was so respected that others would ask permission before doing an act. Sometimes Toppa would let them know they didn't need his permission. At other times, they would come to Toppa for advice. Toppa had his way of giving them hope despite being locked up and denied their freedom. Toppa always reminded the chickens that they were all brothers and sisters and encouraged them to live in love and unity. He told them if they were to gain their freedom from humans, they needed to work together and be at peace if they wanted to escape.

Typically, each bird in the enclosure had a pen. Toppa's pen was the biggest and the most comfortable. Usually, three hours after breakfast, they are allowed to take walks outside their pen in the big compound of the enclosure. This often allowed them to interact more with one another. While in the compound, the workers would clean the pens and ensure the water was replaced. Afterward, they would be ordered to return to their pen.

They enjoyed this period which they could mix up a lot. Some of the cocks use this period to bond with some hens.

Some even fall in love during this period. This made some of them patiently wait for this period after breakfast. During this period, they also had time to stay around Toppa; they all wanted to stay around Toppa because Toppa was the boss and was an exciting cock to be around. Whenever they saw Toppa, they would bend their heads to show respect.

During the waiting period, while everyone was

still waiting for a new fight date to be announced, Toppa's master brought in two giant Jamaican cocks. One was called Snowbowl, and the other Jack. Jack was Snowbowl's younger brother but was stronger, so he had his brother's respect. Once Jack and Snowbowl entered the enclosure, they dominated the others. They did everything together, and wherever they found themselves, they turned heads and demanded a lot of respect from the birds around them. No one wanted to get on their bad side as their size alone was terrifying. They were also ruthless and mischievous. Their previous master got rid of them because they killed too many comrades. They would kill birds for something as simple as not greeting them in the morning. Whenever they killed their comrade, they ate its flesh; their previous owners only returned to find bones and feathers remains. They had been counseled and even punished occasionally, but their actions remained the same. Their previous master they were better off sold.

Toppa's master bought them because of their strength and size. What he wasn't aware of was their history. He had heard about the Jamaican cocks and the many fights they won. So, he boarded a plane to Jamaica and declared his interest in buying them. He thought it would be a good investment until they started to kill off his birds. In the short time, they were in the enclosure, he had already lost much money.

When Jack and Snowbowl entered the enclosure, they didn't know who Toppa was because their previous owners didn't allow them to watch TV. Toppa's master had a big TV in the enclosure, which all the birds could watch and be entertained when bored. On the first day, after breakfast, they remained seated and watched how things worked in the enclosure. They noticed Toppa had the biggest cage, but they didn't know why. Toppa looked very simple and like every other cock. Then it was time for the birds to be released into the compound. Upon release, Jack and Snowbowl saw most birds walking immediately towards Toppa's pen, waiting for Toppa to come out. When he did, they followed him. Jack and Snowbowl, of course, didn't like this. They wanted to be the ones in charge. "I can't understand why they are all following that cock," Snowbowl said disgustingly. "We must change the narrative here as soon as possible," Jack said. "I don't see what's so special about him?" Snowbowl said. "I think maybe he got some charisma. Cocks that have charisma always attract a lot of attention."

Just that moment, another cock passed them and barely noticed them as they stood before their pen. He was rushing to greet Toppa. "Hey, you there, come here!" Snowbowl yelled at the surprised cock. The cock turned and saw the two Jamaican cocks. "What are you doing? Can't you bow to the great Jack of all cocks?" Snowbowl asked in anger. The cock was confused. Snowbowl moved toward him and angrily kicked him. The cock flew into the air, hit its back on the enclosure wall, and broke one of its wings. This got the attention of some of the other cocks. But Toppa was so busy with the other cocks that he didn't notice what was happening. The next day, Snowbowl and Jack injured two other cocks that had failed to greet them. They broke the leg of one and broke the wing of another. The news about their brutality started spreading gradually in the enclosure.

That night while all the other birds were asleep, Toppa and the Chinese cock got the talking. "Hey, have you heard about Jack and Snowbowl?" The Chinese cock asked Toppa. Toppa thought for a short time. "Those names are very strange. I have never heard of them before," Toppa responded. "Well, they are both here, and they are causing a lot of harm to the other birds," the Chinese cock said. Toppa remained quiet as he pondered what his friend had just told him. Toppa always tried to give everyone the benefit of the doubt. "I know what you are thinking, but that is not it," the Chinese cock said. "These cocks are brutes; they enjoy subjecting other birds around them to torture. I think you must do something about them before they do any further damage," the Chinese cock said to Toppa. Toppa remained quiet and didn't say anything. After a short while, Toppa drifted off to sleep.

The next day the birds in the enclosure were freed from their pens. Toppa was sleepy, so he didn't come out immediately. After the pens were opened, the workers would return an hour later to clean them and replace their water before lunch. While Toppa was sleeping, he heard some noise in the compound, but he was so sleepy it felt more like a dream. The noise continued, but Toppa continued to sleep.

"Toppa! Toppa!" Toppa kept hearing a cock calling out. It sounded like Toppa's friend, the voice of the Chinese cock. The Chinese cock was standing in front of the door calling Toppa. When Toppa didn't respond, he went into

Toppa's pen. "Toppa!" he shouted. Topp opened its eyes and stared at his friend. "How can you be sleeping when a cock is losing its life?" The Chinese cock said. Toppa was lost for a while, and it couldn't understand what the Chinese cock was saying. The Chinese cock could see that Toppa didn't quite understand what was happening. After all, Toppa had just woken up from his sleep.

"Snowbowl and Jack are killing a cock right now," the Chinese cock said to Toppa. Toppa jumped to his feet immediately. He could see all the birds in the enclosure standing in a big circle and watching. Toppa flew down from his pen. The Chinese cock followed behind Toppa. Toppa entered the crowd of birds and walked into the center. The Chinese cock followed and stood behind Toppa. Snowbowl and Jack had already killed the cock and were eating its flesh.

The cock had refused to bend its head before them. After they were freed from their pen, the cock rushed to meet a hen it had fallen in love with. Its mind was so focused that it didn't even notice Snowbowl and Jack. Snowbowl yelled at the cock and asked it to bend its head before them, but the cock ignored them and continued towards his hen-friend. Jack through the cock into the air and against the wall. Then he and Snowbowl used their beaks to tear it apart and fed on its flesh.

"What have you done?" Toppa shouted at Snowbowl and Jack. Every bird in the enclosure was silent and watched what would happen next. "We decide how things work here, not you!" Snowbowl said as he looked at Toppa in anger. "You just killed a fellow cock," said Toppa. "That is against what we practice here. Here, we are all brothers and sisters, and we are our brothers and sisters' keepers. We are properly fed, so there is no need to kill our comrades. What you have done is wicked and uncalled for," Toppa scolded the Jamaican cocks.

Jack became very angry as he didn't like that Toppa was talking like he was the boss. Jack walked towards Toppa and stood in front of him. Jack was much bigger than Toppa. He looked down at Toppa angrily, "Who are you to tell me what to do and what not to do here?" Jack asked in anger. At that moment, every bird in the enclosure was expecting a fight. They knew that Toppa was a good fighter, but they were frightened by the size of Jack and his brother, Snowbowl. If Jack were to win against Toppa, they would suffer in captivity. Even though their master had kidnapped and locked them up against their will, they still had some freedom. They knew they would lose some freedoms should Jack beat Toppa in combat.

Snowbowl walked and stood behind Jack. The Chinese cock was still standing behind Toppa. "We are comrades. I don't think we must fight," Toppa said. But Jack grabbed Toppa and threw him to the side of the enclosure. Every bird in the enclosure was surprised and frightened. If Toppa were to lose to Jack, they would be in real trouble.

The Chinese cock rushed towards Toppa. "Are you okay?" The Chinese cock asked Toppa. Toppa nodded in affirmation. "Move aside and stay out of this," Toppa said to the Chinese cock. The Chinese cock wanted to help take out Snowbowl, but Toppa didn't want to see him hurt. Toppa stood to his feet and glared at Jack and Snowbowl in anger. The Chinese cock stepped away to maintain little distance from Toppa as he had never seen him that angry.

Toppa thought about the hawk he had killed in the past. He knew the giant hawk was far stronger and bigger than Jack and Snowbowl. "It is too weak. Finish it," Jack said to Snowbowl. Snowbowl charged toward Toppa as he got closer and lifted his leg to stomp on Toppa. Toppa managed to grab Snowbowl's two legs which caused it to break. Snowbowl shouted in pain. Jack was shocked to see Snowbowl was lying on the ground in pain. All the other birds were in dismay but quiet.

"My legs! My legs are broken," Snowbowl cried in pain. Jack angrily charged at Toppa. "I'm going to tear you to pieces!" he yelled at Toppa. Toppa remained where he was standing as Jack advanced with great force. and it was now about using its beak on Toppa. Suddenly Toppa counterattached used his beak to pierce Jack's eye. Blood gushed as Toppa grabbed one of Jack's wings and broke it. Jack shouted in pain and fell to the ground.

Everyone started shouting in joy. They rushed and raised Toppa into the air. Everyone was so happy. The workers heard the noise from within the enclosure and wanted to know what was happening. They rushed into the enclosure and found Jack and Snowbowl lying on the ground while the other birds celebrating. Then they saw the remains of the cock Jack and Snowbowl were eating earlier. They were surprised at all that happened within the few minutes the birds were out of their pens. They weren't sure what happened, but they had seen Jack and Snowbowl bully some of the birds in the enclosure in the past. The workers called one of the cocks and asked it what happened. The cock told them Snowbowl and Jack had been bullying some of the birds in the enclosure. The cock also told them that Snowbowl and Jack had killed one of the cocks and were feeding on its flesh when Toppa came to stop them. This caused them to attack Toppa, who fought to defend them. The workers immediately reported the incident to Toppa's master.

Toppa's master called in an ambulance, and they took Snowbowl and Jack to the vet. They stayed at the vet for two days to be properly treated for their injuries. Their broken legs and wings took a long time to heal, but Jack's eye was permanently damaged. The veterinarian that treated them told Toppa's master that while the legs and wings would eventually heal, Jack's eye was permanently damaged. After the treatment, Toppa's master took them to the enclosure and didn't feed them for a whole day as punishment for killing the other birds. The next day, they were fed, but they couldn't come out of their pen because of their injuries. Jack couldn't fly properly because of its broken wing, while Snowbowl couldn't walk because his legs were broken. The birds in the enclosure were relieved that even though they were in captivity, they didn't have to be subjected to further slavery. They were so happy that Toppa came to their rescue. The encounter made them respect Toppa even more than they did before.

Toppa's fight with the Snowbowl and Jack, they realized that being strong wasn't measured by size. Though Toppa looked very little before Jack and Snowbowl, Toppa could defeat both. The experience motivated them a lot.

CHAPTER 10

HUMAN INJUSTICE

It had been three days since Damian returned to the stakeout spot. The TV people had reduced how they talked about Toppa and the Korean cock's fight. Damian grew concerned about whether the Korean cock would recover. It was starting to appear that they might need to devise a new plan to rescue Toppa. He was bored, bored from staying in one spot and watching TV all day. So Damian decided to fly around the neighborhood and make new friends among the hawks.

While Damian flies around, he notices how much respect they have for some lower-class animals than they do for others—particularly dogs and cats. Humans treated them like kings in human territories. They bathe them, feed them, prepare a nice place to sleep, and do all manner of stuff to make them happy. Damian had no idea humans could be that nice to animals. Whenever a dog or a cat was treated wrongly, it was reported to the police.

When Damian returned to his hideout, he noticed a dog owner who often treated their dog poorly. The dog always looked so sad that even Damian took pity on it. There were times when the dog would go without food. So he and Damian would compete for the food scraps the humans dropped. But the dag would usually get there before Damian. This would stir anger in Damian, who usually forgives the dog.

One day, the police came and arrested the owner of the dog because the dog died due to the lousy way the owner of the dog was treating it. Neighbors reported the incident to the police, and the police came and arrested the dog owner. This demonstrated the value humans place on dogs which is also true for cat owners. Cats and dogs were treated with a lot of respect, yet not so much birds, and never liked allowing birds to be free. Damian never saw a cock or a hen that moved about freely. They were always locked up in cages. The ones that flew in the sky humans would hunt them and use them for meat. The only good thing is that cocks and hens kept in cages had time to enjoy good meals. However, their days were numbered as they would end up on some human's plate.

It would break Damian's to see the dead cocks and hens lying on tables at the market. He wouldn't quite stomach how humans would slit their throats without sympathy. Then the chickens would bleed until they drained from them. The same was true for pigeons – some would fly while others were trapped in a small pen in the market. To humans, birds were just a source of food, and if they didn't kill them, they would continue to steal their eggs. Damian saw humans selling the eggs at the market. This angered Damian, as these innocent chicks would never be born into the world.

Then there were the ones who used birds for sport, watching them fight to the death. They would fight to the delight of many people watching for entertainment. They would watch as birds, who should be comrades, fight until one kills the other. Humans made a lot of money using birds for entertainment. It didn't matter the type of bird, humans treated them cruelly, and Damian couldn't understand why.

But Damian birds were not the only lower-class animals suffering at the hands of humans. Just as humans killed birds with no mercy, they did the same to fish, pigs, goats, and cows. Damian wondered, what if all these animals united to fight the humans? Achieving this would be a challenging thing. It would take time to unite all these animals suffering cruelty from humans. It would need one to travel a lot to different territories and meet these animals and discuss with them, but even if they agree to do that, they still have a big problem. Humans had many weapons they used to protect themselves.

The knife that killed birds was something that Damian feared a lot. Damian saw how it slit the throats of some birds without having any mercy on them. The edge was very sharp; the thought of that knife around Damian's neck sent some shivers through Damian's spine. The humans also had cutlasses and swords. These knives were longer and bigger than the ones they used to kill birds and just as dangerous. Damian saw how they were used in crushing the body parts of birds that had bones in them.

Then there were the weapons humans called guns. Humans didn't need to get close to use this weapon. They would just stay at a single spot and fire it without much stress, and the bullet would hit whatever was in the way. Damian believed the gun was the deadliest among them. Some humans used it to kill birds flying in the sky. With knives, birds flying in the sky didn't have to worry much because humans couldn't reach them. However, this was not the case with guns. No matter how far in the sky where they were, humans could shoot them down with guns. This kind of made Damian so scared when Damian was flying around and touring the human territory; Damian knew that it could be exposed to the risk of being shot down with a gun by humans.

All the animals met and understood that freeing themselves from the humans was going to be an easy feat. First, they needed to steal all the human's weapons before fighting their way out of oppression. Then there was the matter of dogs. Dogs were humans' greatest friends. They bonded with humans, so much so that they would protect their owners. Some won't even allow anyone to get close.

A man was living near Damian's hideout. He was always drunk, stumbling his way home.

Watching would always make Damian laugh uncontrollably. Whenever Damian was bored at night, he would wait for this man to return. It was pure entertainment watching stumble all over the place. He had a dog named Lucky who loved him so much, always happy to be around his company. Damian, on some occasions, watched as this man brought home all sorts of for his Lucky. One day Damian attempted to eat some of Lucky's food, but Lucky's aggression scared the living life out of Damian. Since that day, Damian never attempted to go close to Lucky again.

One day Lucky's owner returned home so drunk he staggered as usual to the door. However, he was so he didn't get further than the front of the door where he slept for the night. Lucky found his owner sleeping on the ground before the house and lay there with him. Two people passed by and saw Lucky's owner lying on the ground in a drunken sleep. They tried to steal from his pocket, but Lucky wouldn't have it and attacked, chasing them as fast as their legs could carry them. So if their plan was going to work, Damian knew dogs would be a very big problem, and they would need a solution.

CHAPTER 11
OUT OF COMA

Damian had been so busy touring the human territory that he lost focus on what he was asked to do. The instruction was for Damian to remain close to watch the TV and get relevant information as soon as it was available about the fight between Toppa and the Korean cock. One night, Damian decided to stay put in his hideout because he was tired. As Damian's eyes grew heavy with sleep, he heard the newscaster mention Toppa and the Korean cock. He quickly perked up, only to realize that he had been a few days behind on the news. It had already been five days since the Korean cock had been out of his coma. Damian had gotten so distracted touring the human territory that he fell short of his duties. If he were focused, these new developments would have already been reported to the king.

The fight between the Korean cock and Toppa would be in one month to allow the Korean cock to recover fully. According to the newscaster, the master of the Korean cock had assured people that his fighter would be ready to take on Toppa just as he did to other opponents in the past. This now meant the King could proceed with his plan to rescue Toppa. Damian quickly gathered himself and set off home at night to inform the King. He knew he needed to make up for the time he had already lost and during the journey home continued to beat up himself.

Damian briefed the King about how the Korean cock came out of a coma and how a date had been set for the fight. "This is good news!" the King exclaimed. "Now we can put a plan in motion. The humans will never cease to amaze me with their technologies and inventions," the king continued. "Humans are very intelligent, and we will need to be extra careful if we are going to succeed at rescuing Toppa." The King proceeded to lay out some details of a plan when Damian suggested not involving too many birds. The king agreed. While acknowledging that humans were superior than they were, the King wanted to teach them a lesson. The humans had many technology and tools at their disposal, so the King knew if they tried to challenge humans face-to-face, they would lose. He would need to outwit them. "We don't need to meet them face to face, and we can't win engaging them in a battle," the King told Damian and others in the room. We must ensure they won't know what we are up to, at least not until it's too late.

"I think getting Toppa out will be the biggest challenge," Damian said.

"You have been very helpful, and I am very grateful," the King said to Damian. "However, I want you to return to the human territory and stay there. You will only return if you have any news that would be useful to the mission. But before you go, spend a few days with your family." Damian acknowledged the king and did as instructed.

Damian left the king's presence and went home to see his family. Later that evening, the king called Toppabling and updated him on the latest news about his father's rescue plan. Toppabling was so happy that the time to rescue its father gradually drew closer. The next day, Toppabling was motivated to train harder than before; he wanted to be prepared. Two days quickly went by, and it was time for Damian to return to the human territory to do his part in ensuring Toppa's rescue would be a success.

CHAPTER 12
THE FIGHT

It was one week before the fight between the Korean cock and Toppa, and Damian was still in the human territory and monitoring the situation of things. The fight was the talk of the town, all over the TVs and radios. Everyone was talking about it.

A few days before, reporters visited the Korean cock's enclosure. They gave us behind the scenes of how the Korean cock was training and preparing for the fight. They showed footage of the Korean cock tearing some giant cocks apart. The Korean cock promised it was going to be the same for Toppa. Damian had never seen anything like that before, so he was scared and even had some doubts that Toppa would be able to defeat the

Korean cock. It was clear that they had resumed feeding it with steroids and cocaine. The Korean cock was back to fighting like a beast. His master had now taken responsibility for feeding him to ensure they didn't encounter another life-threatening mistake, which was ironic since one would deem taking steroids and cocaine to be life-threatening.

The same reporters also went to interview and give behind-the-scenes of Toppa's training. They found Toppa sleeping inside its cage when they got to the enclosure. They were disappointed because the fight was just a week away, and Toppa seemed not too bothered. They knew Toppa was a great fighter, but it was interesting enough for airtime. Toppa had never lost any fight, but the Korean cock was not to be disregarded as not a threat. The newscaster saw this as a potential loss for Toppa. This caused Toppa's master to grow concerned that he tried to persuade him into extra training, but Toppa refused. Such an act would normally cause Toppa's master to punish Toppa, but he was afraid that Toppa would get injured, which would reduce their chances of winning the fight. Unknown to them, Toppa practiced inside his cage at night while all the other birds were sleeping.

Four days before the fight, Damian was now

back in hawk territory. The King and everyone were all ready to rescue Toppa. "We will be leaving tomorrow morning. Remember, humans are very intelligent, so we need to be diligent for our plans to work. Damian, Toppabling, two soldiers, and I will be the only ones going for the mission," the king announced. The rest of the birds were disappointed. They all wanted to be part of the mission but couldn't defy the king's order. The next day, the king, Damian, Toppabling, and two soldiers flew off to human territory. They arrived the day before the fight and stayed at Damian's hideout. The king could watch TV and was even more amazed at human accomplishments.

It was fight day, and Toppa stood in the ring covered by a long square net. The top of the net was not covered. The Korean cock was walking towards the ring. The noise was thunderous as people poured in to watch the long-awaited fight between Toppa and the Korean cock.

Toppa was deemed the underdog, with everyone favoring the Korean cock winning the match. Even Toppa's master had already lost confidence in him and decided to kill Toppa after the match and use him for meat should he lose the match. The Korean cock was now standing before Toppa and jumping from one part of the ring to another. Toppa remained in one spot. The entrance to the net was closed. The whistle blew to signify the start of the fight.

The Korean cock immediately charged after Toppa. But didn't expect Toppa's counterattack. Toppa then jumped to meet the Korean cock in the air and kicked the Korean cock's belly, causing him to land on the ground hurt. The rule was that no help should be rendered to any participants in the fight. Everyone was shocked. While the Korean cock was still trying to recover from Toppa's blow, Toppa continued attacking. He used his beak to pierce the Korean cock's eye, blinding him. Everyone was silent. It wasn't the fight that they were expecting. The Korean cock tried to get up, but Toppa did a backflip, turned into the air, and landed a kick that sent him flying. The Korean cock fell to the floor of the ring and died.

Toppa's master was filled with joy. Everyone was shocked, and then the disappointment of betting against Toppa started. This was the moment Toppa was waiting for. While everyone was distracted, Toppa quickly escaped the cage. Toppa's master caught him out of the side of his eye, climbed the net cage, and quickly grabbed his gun. He released the trigger, but Yoppa's friend — the Chinese cock jumped in the way of the bullet.

As the bullet hit the Chinese cock he fell into the net cage. Toppa jumped back into the cage to help his friend. "You have to leave here now," the Chinese cock said to Toppa as it struggled to breathe, "I am lucky to meet a great being like you," the Chinese cock added. Toppa was now sobbing. "I will never forget what you did for me today," Toppa said as he kissed the forehead of the Chinese cock. The Chinese cock died.

By now, everyone's attention was center stage and confused about what was happening. Toppa stood up with an angry look and looked towards his master. He again started climbing out of the cage. Toppa's master aimed his gun to shoot, but Toppabling flew into the air and threw one of the twelve light razor feathers gifted by the king at Toppa's master's neck. Upon impact, the gun fell out of his hand, and he fell to the floor. Everyone started to run frantically.

Toppa and Toppabling's eyes found each other. Without being told, Toppa knew that Toppabling was his son. Tears of joy started to flow from Toppa's eyes, and he couldn't believe he had just seen his son for the first time. The king then flew to the top of the net and threw a rope to Toppa, who caught it. The two soldiers and Damian gave the king a hand as they pulled Toppa out of the cage.

Somehow a fire broke out, so Toppa headed to the enclosure where he was held captive and freed all the birds before flying off with his son.

After flying for about an hour, Toppa, the King, Toppablong, and the King's soldiers stop for a rest. Toppa and Toppabling stared at each other and then hugged each other. "I'm sorry, son, that I couldn't protect your mom," Toppa said to Toppabling.

"Thank you, Father, for being alive!" Toppabling said. Toppa then turned to the king, "Thank you, my dear friend, for taking good care of my son."

"He is my son, too," the king responded.

Pow, pow!!! There were gunshots. Everyone was frightened. Suddenly, Toppa fell to the ground. Toppabling rushed to him and saw that he was bleeding. Toppa was shot. "Dad!" Toppabling cried out. "You have to go. You must escape", Toppa told them as he struggled to breathe. "We can't leave you here, Dad," Toppabling cried. Toppa held the king's hand, "Please, continue to look after my son; he might look huge, but he is still a boy," Toppa said. The king nodded in affirmation as a tear rolled down his cheek. They could hear fast footsteps approaching. "You have to go. Leave me here and go!" Toppa mustered as he looked into the eyes of Toppabling. Topp's breathing was labored, and within seconds, he was no longer breathing. "Dad! Dad!" Toppabling shouted as he shook Toppa. Toppabling started crying uncontrollably, "I will avenge you. I will never let this pass," Toppabling said as he continued to cry.

"I will kill them all, and that's a promise," Toppabling shouted as the king grabbed him. "We must go, son. They are right behind us. Your father is dead. Let's go," the king pulled Toppabling. 'No!" shouted Toppabling. "I am not leaving him here!" The king's guard saw they would die if they didn't leave, so he knocked Toppabling out, tossed him over his shoulder, and took him away — leaving Toppa's body lying there.

TO BE CONTINUED...

About the Author

Dean Duvantie Wilson is a serial entrepreneur and financial coach from Hartford, Ct. He co-founded JAH Financial Services & Real Estate, a business solutions firm, and owns Golden Touch Personal Care and the Josette and Dean Wilson Foundation. Through their foundation, Dean teaches aspiring entrepreneurs and small businesses how to empower others, propelling them toward success and prosperity. Dean is also an author, visionary, and philanthropist who is committed to making a positive impact in the world. With a wealth of experience in Commercial Real Estate, Dean has successfully invested in numerous projects within this domain. His full-service CPA Firm offers a comprehensive range of services, including IRS tax resolution, personal and corporate income tax preparation, estate taxes, payroll, bookkeeping services, business funding, insurance and retirement services, and assistance with US

Citizenship and Immigration. Dean's background is quite diverse; he is an expert in CAA Forensic, a certified money broker, and holds licenses as a life and health insurance agent, public notary, 10X trainer, travel agent, and accountant. His impressive skills and knowledge make him an invaluable asset to any business that seeks to grow and achieve financial success.

Dean is driven by an unwavering passion to effect meaningful change in the lives of others. Whether through my philanthropic initiatives, expertise in Commercial Real Estate, or the range of comprehensive services offered by J.A.H. Financial Service & Real Estate. Dean also takes immense pride in being a devoted father to four wonderful children: two delightful little girls and two handsome young men. He feels fortunate to be married to the epitome of selflessness, Mrs. Josette Hill-Wilson, who has been an extraordinary inspiration throughout my life.

www.ingramcontent.com/pod-product-compliance
Lightning Source LLC
Chambersburg PA
CBHW071947190726
48293CB00004B/1392